810467

Murphy, Shirley Rousseau

Mrs. Tortino's return to the sun

	DATE		

© THE BAKER & TAYLOR CO.

MRS. TORTINO'S
RETURN TO THE SUN

MRS. TORTINO'S

LOTHROP, LEE & SHEPARD BOOKS
New York

810467

RETURN TO THE SUN

by Shirley and Pat Murphy
pictures by Susan Russo

To Louise Gurley Murphy

Library of Congress Cataloging in Publication Data.   Murphy, Shirley Rousseau. Mrs. Tortino's return to the sun.   SUMMARY: Mrs. Tortino finds a way to preserve her family's Victorian home amidst the city's tall new buildings   [1. City and town life–Fiction.   2. Dwellings–Fiction] I. Murphy, Patrick John, (date)– joint author.   II. Russo, Susan.   III. Title   PZ7.M956Mi   [E]   ISBN 0-688-41921-6   ISBN 0-688-51921-0 lib. bdg.   79-20694

Mrs. Tortino lived in an old Victorian house crowded all around by tall, new buildings—fifteen, twenty, even twenty-five stories high. Her mother had lived in that house, her mother before her, and her mother before *her,* and Mrs. Tortino had vowed she would never leave it. But life had become difficult.

The tall buildings made her old house dark. Mrs. Tortino saw the sun rise just before lunch and set again in early afternoon. All the rest was hidden behind gleaming office buildings and glass-walled apartment towers.

The darkness made her garden damp and unhealthy. Her vegetables became droopy and her flowers wouldn't bloom. Even the chestnut tree looked withered.

Then there was the traffic. Its noise was a constant din, and Mrs. Tortino's old cat, Pursifur, had gotten the wheezes from the terrible gas fumes. He spent his time on the roof, where the air was fresher, but not much, and the sun was a little closer, but not much. And still he wheezed.

But in spite of the dark, and the smog, and Pursifur's wheezing, and the wilted flowers, and the impatient horns, and strangers staring through her windows, Mrs. Tortino would not move from the house where her mother had lived, and her mother before her, and her mother before her. When people came with money to buy it, so they could tear it down and construct an insurance building or a bank or a hotel in its place, Mrs. Tortino turned them away with angry words.

Instead, she took tender care of the old house, repairing the plumbing when it leaked and replacing the pipes when they rusted in the damp air. She kept the walls freshly painted inside and out and mended the foundation whenever cracks began to appear. She even packed away her good china, for the rumble of trucks jarred it on the shelf.

It grew smoggier and noisier as more buildings rose nearby. The traffic became an endless snarl and Pursifur gave up the rooftop for fresher air inside.

Now even more people stopped to trample Mrs. Tortino's garden, leave trash in it, and pull up her flowers. She sent them all away.

Then one day in early spring, a little man in a bowler hat came to her door. Somehow he seemed different from the others. He walked all around her shaded house. He examined her early lettuce and her tomato plants. He tilted up the young flowers for a better look. He scratched Pursifur's back until the old cat swooned.

He looked at the shadows that lay thick across the roof and the garden. He sniffed the foul air and glared, with Mrs. Tortino, at a brash young couple peering in through her parlor window. He noted that the only birds in the garden were a pair of cross, bedraggled sparrows, nesting in her chestnut tree.

Then he leaned close, and whispered something in Mrs. Tortino's ear. She scowled. So he *was* just like all the rest, offering her money for her home.

But wait, there was more. Mrs. Tortino listened, her eyes opening wide. "Could you really do that?" she asked.

The little man nodded.

"A tall building right where my house stands, but you won't destroy...?"

"That's right," he said. "Your house will be under the same patch of sky, on the same street, at the same address. You'll keep your chestnut tree, your grumpy sparrows, your flowers and vegetables, and Pursifur. Everything."

"And there will be money for more tomato plants and some nasturtium seed and sardines for Pursifur?"

"Indeed," said the little man, smiling. "A lifetime's supply."

Mrs. Tortino stared at the man in the bowler hat for a long time. Then, at last, she said, "All right!" And they shook hands.

When he had gone, Mrs. Tortino looked down at Pursifur. "Isn't it amazing?" she said. "I can hardly believe it's possible!"

Pursifur just hummed quietly.

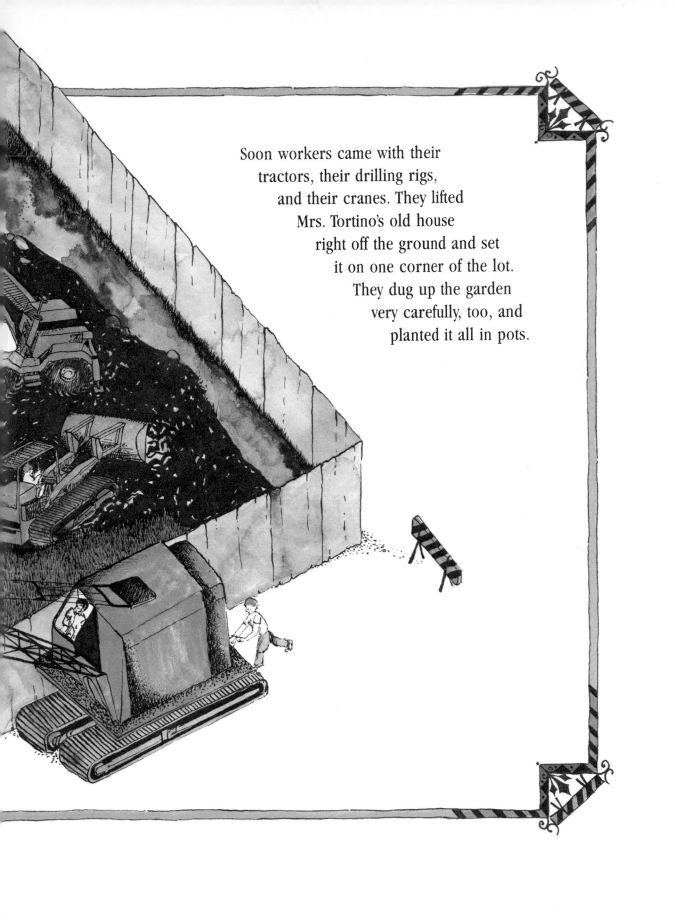

Soon workers came with their
tractors, their drilling rigs,
and their cranes. They lifted
Mrs. Tortino's old house
right off the ground and set
it on one corner of the lot.
They dug up the garden
very carefully, too, and
planted it all in pots.

Now the digging could begin. They scooped a deep hole for the new foundation. Then they drilled even deeper holes and filled these with cement.

After five weeks, the foundation was complete and a strong steel frame had been built above it, two stories high. On top of the frame stood a crane. And next to the crane stood Mrs. Tortino's family home. Her chestnut tree hung beside it in a washtub. Her flowers, and lettuce, and some young beets and spinach all dangled in pots that swung from the metal I beams and cross-beams and scaffolding. Already more sun came in.

The only people, now, to peer into her parlor were the welders and the riveters who were building the metal frame. They showed her how to weld and how to rivet, while Mrs. Tortino served them afternoon tea on her cozy front porch.

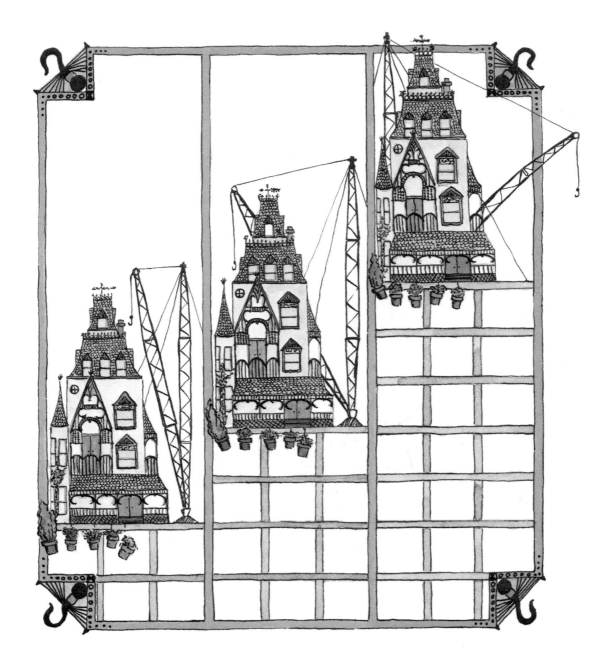

Every week, as a new floor was finished, Mrs. Tortino's house was lifted higher. From the second floor to the fourth. From the fourth to the seventh. Each time it rose, the sunshine increased, the air grew fresher, and Pursifur wheezed less. The flowers stood straighter. The tomato vines climbed madly. The beets and spinach grew to record size. And Mrs. Tortino smiled broadly.

Now she trotted along the I beams and rode down the construction elevator
in order to go to market.

She pulled her morning paper up on a cord that grew longer and longer as
the house rose. And at night she lowered her garbage to the street.

She hung her laundry from the scaffolding, startling the office workers next
door.

Pursifur watched it all from the safety of the window ledge.

Below, on the first floors, the walls were now being built. Bricklayers and plumbers and electricians had joined the crew. And they, too, met on Mrs. Tortino's porch for afternoon tea.

By the twentieth week, Mrs. Tortino's house was seventeen stories off the ground, where it was sunny from five in the morning until nine at night. The tomatoes were thick on the vines. The corn was tall. And the squash was bigger than Pursifur. Mrs. Tortino hardly knew there were cars below unless she leaned outside to look.

And each time the house was lifted, what a ride!

At first she had cringed in her bed when the great crane picked up her old home. Then she had taken to looking out the window. At last she simply plunked down on the front porch and rocked to the swinging motion as her house was hoisted higher in the sky. It was like being on a ferris wheel.

By the twenty-seventh week, Mrs. Tortino lived twenty-four stories above the street, where the air was as smooth as whipped cream and the sun so bright that she bought the first parasol she had owned since she was a girl.

Even the sparrows seemed happier and had hatched their second batch of eggs. Now other birds, grackles and pigeons, came to her garden, and sometimes an owl. And in the moonlight, nighthawks hunting insects swooped above her rooftop.

Then at last, just before Thanksgiving, when the last of the garden was ready to harvest and the air was growing chill, the new building was finished. It was the tallest in the city. Thirty floors. And people looking up from below said, "Why, the Equity Building has a penthouse on top." Others looked through powerful glasses and said, "I believe I see pumpkins up there! Aren't those cornstalks and squash? And isn't that a chestnut tree?"

Certainly there was a chestnut tree as well as the largest pumpkins Mrs. Tortino had grown in years. But it was not a penthouse they saw. It was Mrs. Tortino's old family home that her mother had lived in, and her mother before her, and her mother before her.

Now no one looked in through Mrs. Tortino's windows any more. No one could. And when she peered down on everyone else, they looked no larger than ants in the dark, narrow street below.

And Pursifur?

Oh, Pursifur doesn't wheeze any longer. In fact, he has grown a trifle fat and lazy, too lazy to chase the birds that flock to Mrs. Tortino's garden. And when the welders, the riveters, the bricklayers, the electricians, and the plumbers come to tea on the third Sunday in June, Pursifur has sardines with *his* tea, beneath the chestnut tree, between the squash and tomatoes, in the warm afternoon sun.